I0537719

SHE-DEVIL
ROCKS

LANCE ERLICK

Finlee Augare Books (Chicago)

This is a work of fiction. All of the characters, organizations, and events portrayed herein are either products of the author's imagination or are used fictitiously, and any similarities to actual persons, organizations, or events is entirely coincidental. Also, though locations used in this work exist, for dramatic effect details have been altered. Accordingly, they should be considered fictitious.

Copyright © 2015 Lance Erlick
All rights reserved, including the right to reproduce this book, or portions thereof, in any form.

Finlee Augare Books, Chicago, IL
ISBN: 978-1-943080-07-6 (print)
ISBN: 978-1-943080-08-3 (e-book)

Printed in the United States of America

The will to overcome

ONE

The private plane hadn't arrived yet. Bradley Munsch fidgeted in the shadows. The rest of his ninth grade class eagerly waited outside the hangar for their ecology field trip to Catalina to begin.

Angry gray clouds poured in to blot out the afternoon sun. It started to rain, which seemed unusual for Los Angeles in June. Hoping it would be a quick sprinkle, Bradley moved closer to his backpack in the hangar to stay dry.

Waiting was the worst part. Each moment their flight delayed was another that Bradley needed to find ways to avoid Malcolm. Two years older than the other boys, Malcolm Montgomery was number one, the tallest boy in the class. God in his infinite humor had seen fit to make Bradley the smallest of thirteen boys though not small enough to escape Malcolm's notice. Making matters worse, Bradley didn't feel lucky as number thirteen. He was safe as long as Ms. Rose was around. Malcolm made sure their teacher never saw his evil twin.

Bradley had done everything he could to avoid this school-sponsored trip. He complained to his dad that his stomach ached, which was true. He had a terrible headache. He even faked an ankle sprain, but nothing worked.

"You've been like this since your mother died," his dad had said. "It's been six months. Stop acting like a wimp."

That ended their little chat. After his mom had died, Bradley's dad had placed him in this school with other boys who had experienced loss. He felt no kinship with the other boys, but his regular public school had been no kinder.

Shielded from their teacher by other boys, Malcolm eyed Bradley alone in the hangar. Covering his eyes from the rain, Bradley hurried around the other boys toward Ms. Rose.

"Everyone under the canopy," she said. Ms. Rose was only slightly taller than Bradley, yet all the boys straightened up when she spoke.

While the others moved under the canopy near the hangar, Malcolm grabbed Danny, number twelve, the second smallest boy, and hammered his arm with a big fist. Danny protected his face with his other hand.

Though five inches shorter, Miguel Ventura stood up to Malcolm. "I'm warning you."

Miguel was the second tallest in the class and had an older brother who roughed him up. Bradley had no brothers or sisters. Instead, he had a father who had introduced him to his belt for sulking or any number of other faults. Bradley swallowed hard.

A small jet taxied toward the private airport office.

"Everyone line up," Ms. Rose said.

As always, they lined up according to height, with Malcolm and Miguel up front and Bradley in thirteenth place. Danny covered the welt on his arm with his hand and hid behind taller boys in front of him.

"Thank you for arranging this fieldtrip," Malcolm said. He flashed the teacher his toothy grin. "This is going to be educational." He flipped back his bushy black hair, revealing lengthening sideburns. A head taller than the rest of the class, he was the only one who could grow thick facial hair.

Smiling, Ms. Rose walked along their ranks to ensure they weren't misbehaving. "I need to check inside to make sure we're cleared to leave on account of the rain. Malcolm's in charge until I return."

Ms. Rose marched into the small airport office. Coach and social studies teacher Mack McDonald was inside talking to a blonde girl who might have been our age. Eyes red, she looked miserable. She flipped curls out of her eyes, jabbed her finger toward Coach, and then toward the class. Bradley couldn't hear what she was saying, but she seemed pretty upset. He hadn't seen her before, but there was something about her that—

Thwack.

Like a baseball bat across the head, the thump sent Bradley sprawling onto the wet concrete out in the rain. He scraped his arm and knee, and prayed this would get him out of the fieldtrip.

"Little Bradley got himself a girlfriend," Malcolm said.

Danny cringed and scooted into the hangar to hide. Miguel followed. The other boys gathered around, watching, thankful that Malcolm's attention wasn't on them.

Bradley could always tell the days that Malcolm's dad belted him or his parents fought. It didn't seem to matter which. On those days, Malcolm looked for trouble, as if that would balance things.

The big boy with the bushy sideburns stood with the sly grin he got while thinking up new ways to show he was number one. "No girl will ever look at you, Little Worm," he said. "That she-devil will turn you into mush. Got it? Leave her to men like me." Malcolm puffed up his chest and flexed his arms.

As long as he was talking, he wasn't hurting anyone. Yet.

"Get up, Little Worm. Maybe you'll get lucky and get

stranded at sea with her. That's the only way she'll ever look at you."

"Yeah, Little Worm," Tony the Joker added. He was number five and our class clown.

"Are there really she-devils?" another asked. It sounded like Jon, number eight and the chubbiest boy in the class. He couldn't help it. Both his parents were big.

Malcolm went to smack Jon. Miguel stepped in and Malcolm moved back, holding up both hands as if surrendering. He dropped his arms, straightened up, and gave his toothy smile.

Coach McDonald hurried out from the airport office, his short hair matted by the rain. "What's going on here?"

Malcolm bowed and stepped back to let Coach through. "Bradley fell," he said in his sweet voice. "I think he needs medical attention."

Coach helped Bradley to his feet, examined the rain-soaked scrapes, and scooped him up in his arms. He carried the boy into the airport office. Bradley felt further humiliated.

The coach set the boy on a sofa and waved his arm toward someone Bradley couldn't see. "You want to tell me what happened?"

Bradley wanted to tell, but his stomach knotted. He didn't want to imagine what else Malcolm could think up.

The blonde girl he'd seen earlier appeared with bandages and ointment. She was slightly taller than Bradley with striking cheekbones. She was very pretty up close, though her eyes were red from crying. She smiled and moved out of sight. He wanted to ask her to return. But he was too nervous to think what to say.

"This doesn't look bad." Coach dabbed the knee with a cotton swab. "Did someone push you?"

"I don't think so," Bradley said, disappointed that his scrapes wouldn't excuse him.

"You can tell me." Coach squeezed ointment on a

bandage and slapped it onto Bradley's knee. Then he moved to the boy's arm.

Bradley looked up at Coach McDonald, who had told the boys to call him Mack. He had a rugged look with a square jaw. He was a tough man who didn't belittle Bradley like his dad did or attack him as Malcolm did.

Mack didn't believe that Bradley's regular bruising came from his being clumsy, but he never saw the worst of them. Bradley's dad had been careful not to leave a mark on arms, legs, or face, and Bradley was careful not to let Coach see his bottom. That wasn't proper. Malcolm hadn't been so careful, but Bradley didn't want more.

Coach ran his fingers through the boy's hair. "You'll be fine. Don't let this spoil your trip. Let it go and move on." He started to help the boy up.

"I can walk."

Coach Mack put his arm over the boy's shoulder and led him outside. The others had escaped the rain and boarded along with their luggage.

When he reached the plane, Bradley looked back to see the girl wave and smile. Bradley waved, smiled back, wishing he'd gotten the nerve to say something to her.

* * *

Coach Mack and Bradley were the last two on the plane. There were a total of fifteen passenger seats, one on each side of the aisle, and a small toilet cabinet in the back. Coach went back to sit beside Ms. Rose. The only other seat was by the door. Bradley took it. Danny, who sat across the aisle, sank as low as he could in his seat.

Malcolm was sitting behind Danny. "Had to make us late," he whispered.

Bradley watched the co-pilot, a late-thirtyish blonde with bouncy curls like the girl in the office. She checked what looked like a weather map. All she had to do was look outside at the gray clouds and rain.

"That she-devil grab your tongue?" Malcolm said.

The co-pilot double-checked the door and stood before them. "We're cleared for takeoff. Is everyone buckled in?"

From the back of the plane, Coach flashed a thumbs up.

"Then we're off. It'll be bumpy; nothing to worry about. It's a very short flight." The co-pilot climbed into her seat and the plane taxied for takeoff.

"Are you giving me your evil eye?" Malcolm asked as the plane lifted into the rain.

Bradley scooted into the corner by the window.

Malcolm leaned forward to see him. "You can't hide. You got a thing for Coach Mack's daughter, don't you?"

Feeling his face burn red, about to explode, Bradley stared out the window. Charcoal clouds darkened by the minute. Lightning hit the wing. He jumped, reached for the door, and stopped at the last moment.

Coach Mack hurried up the aisle and leaned over Danny. "Why don't you go sit with Ms. Rose?"

Danny looked relieved to be away from Malcolm. He hurried back.

Coach took Bradley's hand. "You need to sit. This storm is nothing to worry about, just a little rain that blew in." He checked that Bradley's seatbelt was tight and sat across the aisle in Danny's vacated seat. He watched Bradley with concern.

At times like this Bradley cursed not being even smaller so he could disappear. He would never hear the end of looking at the girl or Coach treating him like a baby by scooping him up in his arms. Bradley bit back tears and stared out the window as the sky grew even darker. Day had turned to night. Bradley hated storms. They reminded him of welts on his bottom the last time he wimped out over a little lightning after his mom had died.

The plane bounced up and dropped. Bradley's stomach was in his throat. He felt ill. Coach held out a bag. "In case you get sick."

"I'm fine," Bradley said, though he felt as sick as he

had when his dad made him eat moldy bread. His dad forgot to buy fresh bread when his mom went into the hospital, and was in a hurry to leave.

"If you need anything, holler," Coach said. He walked up to the cockpit and whispered to the co-pilot.

Malcolm scooted up to the seat Coach had left and glared at Bradley. "We're taking you to She-devil Island. You wet your pants yet?"

For the first time that Bradley could recall, Ms. Rose caught Malcolm's evil twin. "That's enough. Go sit in the back, in my seat."

Looking ready to defy her, Malcolm remained seated. He clenched his fists on the armrest. His eyes tightened. His evil twin fought for control. Then he put on a smile and stood up. "Whatever you say, Ms. Rose."

She sat across from Bradley in the seat Malcolm had just been in.

Malcolm headed back then returned. While blocking their teacher's view, he placed a heavy hand on Bradley's shoulder and squeezed. "I'm sorry, Ms. Rose. I don't know what came over me. It's the storm and flying and all."

"We'll talk later," Ms. Rose said. "Sit in the back and fasten your seatbelt."

Malcolm bowed, sticking his large rear end into Bradley's face. He let loose what smelled like rotten eggs. "I need to tell Coach Mack something urgent. Then I'll sit in the back of the plane like a good boy."

"Make it quick."

Malcolm shared his evil-twin face with Bradley and squeezed into the cockpit area by Coach Mack. Bradley stared outside at rain hammering the wing and the ocean below. He prayed for this to quickly end.

The plane bounced up, down, and then right. Bradley waited for the aircraft to level out and his nervous stomach to settle down. Instead the plane dived like he'd seen in dog-fight video games. Only this wasn't a game.

Something shifted, maybe their bags in cargo beneath

them. Lights blinked out. Lightning flashed outside. The plane turned left then right, dove, and nosed up. When it did, Coach Mack flew down the aisle like a loose ball. A sickening crunch of metal, plastic, and bone came from the back of the plane where he landed. Groans followed. Ms. Rose got up and carefully walked back, holding tight to each seat.

Malcolm clung to an aluminum handle that had kept him from falling. With his sly grin, he looked ready to pounce on Bradley now that Ms. Rose had gone.

Gripping the armrests, the smaller boy stared outside. Through the rain, seas boiled not far beneath them. A wall of land appeared up ahead coming right toward them. It didn't seem real, as if he was watching a video game. He curled his feet up under him and gripped the armrests.

The plane nosed up and slapped down like a fly swatter, throwing Bradley forward until he thought his seatbelt would cut him in half. The plane flipped upward. Metal squealed, plastic snapped. Suddenly, the cockpit was at a ninety-degree angle to the cabin. Then it was gone.

At some point Malcolm had moved to the seat beside Bradley. He ducked his head down, drew his feet up, and clung to his seatbelt. Fear had replaced his sly grin. He cringed as Bradley did before getting a beating.

Bradley looked away and tucked his body into a tight fist, covering his face with his hands. The fuselage tumbled onto its back, sliding backwards and upside down. Bradley hung from his seat, the belt digging into his churning stomach.

Windows blew out. The plane skidded through shrubs. The cabin split apart, scattering seats and passengers like bowling pins. Bradley's seat fell loose, hit the top of the headrest, and landed on its back. The seat skidded to a stop on a sandy beach. His head had missed the ground because he was so short.

Metal and other seats scattered around him. Angry waves pounded rocks nearby.

His heart raced until he thought it would explode. Heavy rains soaked him. The storm made it dark as night.

Bradley unfastened his seatbelt and rolled out onto the sand. He threw up. His stomach threatened to rip apart from pressing against the seatbelt. He ached all over and wondered what he'd broken. His foot hurt as if he'd twisted it.

Up the hill where the cockpit had broken off, lightning struck. Something sparked. An explosion followed and then fire.

Shaking, he got to his feet to look around. His foot shot out pain, more like stubbing his toe than a sprain, though.

Nearby, crawling out from under his seat was Miguel, the only boy who dared to stand up to Malcolm. He made guttural groans, got to his feet, and limped in a circle. His right hand twitched. Screams and moans rang out all around.

Number four Seth's head lay at an awkward angle beneath his seat. Bradley pushed him onto his back. Seth's head flopped to the side as if he were asleep. His mouth gaped open. Bradley hurried away. He stumbled onto two more boys who weren't moving. Then he spotted Coach Mack, his arms and legs at odd angles, his head dented in. He lay still on the beach. Bradley held his hand over Coach's mouth and felt no breathing.

The plane's toilet had landed on number six, Tad. Bradley tried to push it away, but couldn't budge it. Holding his stomach, he looked for Ms. Rose.

TWO

In a daze, Bradley walked past Tony the Joker, who mumbled to himself as he tried to undo his seatbelt. Bradley helped Danny out of his and then checked on the others. Numbers nine and ten lay on the ground twisted beneath their seats. Their necks looked broken. Bradley's stomach tumbled like a clothes drier. Waves crashed to his right. He froze.

Ms. Rose lay on her back, her hair matted, and her head on a rock. Malcolm leaned over her, giving her mouth-to-mouth. She wasn't moving.

Barely able to see through the rain and darkness, Bradley walked up the beach. He wiped his eyes. If Ms. Rose was gone then Malcolm was in charge. Malcolm wanted him dead. He'd said so only last week. Malcolm later said he was only trying to get a reaction, but Bradley wasn't so sure.

Several boys joined Malcolm by Ms. Rose. They looked scared. Bradley wandered, raindrops filling his eyes. Miguel clutched his right elbow and tried to stretch. He looked to be in a lot of pain. He was Bradley's only hope if there were no adults.

"Any idea where we are?" Jake asked rubbing his

shoulder. He was the third tallest in the class and a fast runner who usually avoided Malcolm's wrath by siding with the bigger boy.

Malcolm let go of Ms. Rose. Her head flopped onto the rock like a wet dishrag. He stood up and glared at Jake. "Do I look like a traffic cop?" He glanced around with a bewildered look on his face, as if he couldn't collect his thoughts. His hands trembled. He kept clenching and unclenching his fists.

"Coach and Ms. Rose didn't make it." Jake's voice sounded shaky. "Five boys are gone." He sounded ready to cry, which was so unlike him. He also limped, holding his right arm.

"Who put you in charge?" Malcolm looked around at the wreckage and then at Jake. He brushed his wet hair out of his eyes.

"I think we need a doctor," Jake said, massaging his arm.

Malcolm looked down at Ms. Rose by his feet. For a moment he acted stumped. Then he glanced at the boys gathering around him. "Ms. Rose put me in charge." He took a deep breath and puffed out his chest. "Well then, we'll call this island She-devil Rocks. That's where we are." He tried to grin but the mask turned into a grimace.

"Not so fast," Miguel said, shuffling over. "If Ms. Rose can't speak for herself, I don't accept you in charge. In fact, I think you did something to crash the plane."

"Really?" Malcolm stepped back. "We're lost at sea and you want to challenge me."

"Maybe we don't like you in charge." Miguel pulled out a pocket knife and opened the blade. He held the weapon in front of him. "Anyone think Malcolm in charge is a good idea?"

Jake gave them room. "Ms. Rose needs a doctor."

"She's dead," Malcolm said. "She said I was in charge. Her last words. That makes it sacred."

Nearby number five, Tony the Joker, wrapped cloth

around his ankle. Bradley half expected him to jump up and say, "Surprise."

Number eight, Jon, kept holding his head as if it were too big for his body. His taller and thinner friend Rick, number seven, had difficulty standing. Danny stumbled around.

"Jake's right," Miguel said, favoring his right leg. He still gripped the knife. "I say we—"

Malcolm approached and held out his hand. "I say let's be partners, then. Let's shake on it."

Miguel stepped back to keep his distance. Stumbling, he swiped his knife at Malcolm and fought to steady himself. Malcolm caught him. Instead of letting go, he grabbed hold of Miguel's right wrist, twisted it, and rammed the knife up into Miguel's chest.

"You dare swing a knife at me," Malcolm yelled. "You dare! You're not my damned mother. You hear me? And you're certainly not my bastard father."

He dropped Miguel to the ground. "See what you've done? See what you've made me do?"

Noticing Jake and the others eyeing the knife, Malcolm took the blade, wiped it off on Miguel's shirt, and placed it in his pocket. "We'll have no more of that." He straightened up and grinned.

Lightning flashed up toward where the cockpit landed. A lone figure stood on the hill above the beach, the last person Bradley would have expected: the blonde girl from the airport, the one who had brought bandages. He started toward her.

Looking like a shaggy dog with his hair matted over his sideburns, Malcolm blocked the way. "No one goes anywhere unless I say so. Everyone gather whatever we can use and bring it to me."

Bradley looked up at the hill. The girl was gone. He hadn't seen her on the plane, hadn't seen how she could have gotten on. His mind must have been playing tricks.

"We should build a fire," Jake said, "or make a sign on the beach. That's what people do."

Malcolm tripped Jake, sending him sprawling onto wet sand. "Ms. Rose put me in charge, not you. I'm number one."

Favoring his right arm, Jake crawled away but didn't get up. "We need to do something so they'll find us and bring a doctor."

Jake looked like he wanted to stand up to Malcolm, but after what happened to Miguel, Bradley doubted anyone would.

Malcolm stood over Jake. "It's too wet to make a fire, you dumb klutz. Besides, the only 'they' going to find us are the she-devils." Malcolm kicked sand at Jake. "You want she-devils gouging out your eyes?"

"Do they do that?" Danny asked.

Bradley wanted to smack number twelve for drawing Malcolm's attention their way. Instead, he moved toward the crashing waves and recalled the first time Malcolm had ranted about she-devils, after a social worker had visited the school. Malcolm had carried on for over a week, but only while Ms. Rose couldn't hear.

Malcolm faked a punch toward Danny, who dropped to the ground, covering his head.

"Anyone else think they should be in charge?" Malcolm asked.

Everyone froze. Bradley held his breath and lowered his profile, hoping Malcolm wouldn't notice him.

Jake stood up, limped, and seemed to be doing better. "We need to let the authorities know where we are so they can help."

Malcolm spun around and stepped back so he could keep the other boys in sight. "Is that what you want? This is a damned sight better adventure than what the school planned. Who needs a stupid old ecology trip when we have all the nature we need right here."

"Malcolm, people are injured," Jake said. He eyed Miguel and stepped back.

"Dead," Malcolm said. "Say it. We have dead people. We'll bury them at sea like pirates do."

Bradley shivered at the word "dead". All four of his grandparents were gone along with his mom. His dad had spared him their funerals, which meant Bradley never got the chance to say goodbye. Seeing Coach Mack, Ms. Rose, and now six boys who weren't moving, Bradley couldn't decide whether his dad had done him a favor. He didn't want to say goodbye to Coach Mack or Ms. Rose. He trembled at the image of what Malcolm had done to Miguel. He was glad it was too dark to see all the blood.

Unable to breathe, Bradley wiped tears from his eyes and moved farther away. He was thankful the rain and dark shielded his eyes. He didn't need to give Malcolm another reason to single him out.

Danny hadn't moved from his spot curled up on the beach, protecting his head.

"I say we build a bonfire and burn the bodies," Tony said. "Then we can catch she-devils and burn them." He swung his arms as if throwing bodies into a fire.

The class clown's attempt at humor was shallow, his voice shaky. Still, the words sent chills up Bradley's spine.

Malcolm walked up to Tony and glowered at him. Then he grinned. "That's what we'll do. We'll build a huge bonfire … in the pouring rain." He punched Tony's shoulder. "Any other bright ideas?"

Numbers seven and eight, Rick and Jon, moved up the hill to get away from Malcolm.

Malcolm threw a stone, hitting Jon's back. "How you planning to guard against she-devils? Your only chance is to stick together and do what I say. Ms. Rose put me in charge."

Bradley looked at their teacher lying in the sand. She still hadn't moved. Her head hung back, her mouth open, gathering rain. Her eyes stared up, vacant. Was this how his mom had looked after she'd died of lung cancer? His lunch threatened to come up.

He looked away.

"We need a boat or something," Jake said. "Head east and we'll find land."

Malcolm grabbed the smaller boy's shirt in his right fist. "We aren't going anywhere. Got it. No fires. No signs. No boats. We're on a nature adventure right here. You with me or against me?"

Jake grabbed hold of Malcolm's arm, but he was no match for the bigger boy. "We stick together, like you say. I just think—"

"Leave the thinking to me. Got it?"

Jake nodded.

"Say "Yes, sir." That's what real people do."

"Yes, sir."

"Okay," Malcolm said. "Jake, you can be my first lieutenant. Your job is to see the others pay attention and follow orders. Can you do that?"

"Yes, sir."

"Good boy." Malcolm clenched his left fist and moved the arm a little. He let his arm go slack and looked at the other boys. "Now, we need a sergeant-at-arms."

"We've got no arms," Tony said, "excepting the ones hanging from our shoulders."

Malcolm swaggered toward the clown and grinned. "You've got the right idea, so I'll name you my sergeant-at-arms."

"What do I get to do?"

"You get to beat on anyone who doesn't obey," Malcolm said.

The big boys, who stood toward the front of the line, were getting ready to gang up on the smaller ones. *Thanks, Ms. Rose.*

"First order is for each of you to gather everything we

can use for our adventure and put it right here." Malcolm used his heel to dig a circle in the sand. "If anyone finds a flashlight, bring it to me."

Bradley glanced up the hill for a glimpse of the girl. She wasn't there. It had to be his imagination distracting him. He moved to a couple of suitcases scattered on the beach. The other boys staked claim to what they'd gathered.

Rick hid behind his friend, fiddling with something. His cell phone. *Of course.* Bradley reached into his pocket. He still had his.

"Hey, hey," Malcolm said. "None of that." He grabbed Rick's cell phone. "We don't get to use these until we've had our adventure and I say so. Lieutenant? Master-at-arms? Gather the cell phones and give them to me." He grabbed Jon's cell.

Jake held out his hand. Bradley considered running instead of giving up his phone. But his foot hurt and he couldn't outrun Jake anyhow. He handed it over. Danny gave his to Tony.

Malcolm dumped the phones into his rain-splashed circle in the sand. "This is a start. Collect phones from the dead people." Being careful with his left arm, he dropped down next to Ms. Rose. He fished around in her pockets and tossed her cell phone on the pile.

Bradley moved behind what was left of the plane's tail. Clothes and suitcases littered the beach out to the waves. He wished he could have kept his phone, though there was no one he wanted to call. His dad would tell him to man up, whatever that meant. His teacher and coach couldn't help. He shed tears for his mom, but she was gone.

"Are you hiding a cell phone?" Malcolm asked, standing over Danny. He reached into the smaller boy's pockets and pulled out Danny's contacts case. Malcolm examined the case as if it could magically turn into a phone. "You'll get this back after you check each body and bag for cell phones. Got it?" He pushed Danny toward Seth, who remained strapped under his seat.

Malcolm kicked the seat, sending it and Seth onto their sides. "There. Find his cell."

Shaking, Danny rummaged through the boy's pockets. Coming up empty, he shrugged and held out his hands.

Number one smacked the wrists. "You failed." He pulled Danny over to the circle filled with cell phones. "Look here. How many do we have?"

Jake tossed another phone onto the pile along with two flashlights. "Thirteen."

Malcolm stopped to do the math. He hadn't tossed his phone in, which meant there was one missing, the one Danny couldn't find. With rain pelting them, Bradley dug into one of the carry-on bags.

"Close enough," Malcolm said. He shoved Danny onto the pile of phones. "Smash them."

"How will anyone find—"

"I'll keep one phone. You destroy the rest." Malcolm picked up a phone and hit Danny across the side of the head.

While everyone else watched Danny curl up on the ground, Bradley found what he was looking for. Seth's jacket had landed under scattered clothes and crushed bags. The boy's cell phone was in the left pocket. Bradley took the phone, stuffed it in his pocket, and hid behind the plane's tail. He was shivering in the rain.

Malcolm picked up the phones one by one and hit exposed parts of Danny's body: head, arm, shoulder. Then he slapped Danny's head.

"Hey! Stop!" Danny yelled. "I can't see. My contact popped out."

Malcolm stood up, as if stunned by Danny's outburst. "That wouldn't have happened if you'd broken the cell phones as I asked. Now get busy."

Danny cowered. "Help me. Jake? Tony?"

Tony wiped his ever-present grin off is face and moved away. Jake looked like he wanted to help, but he took one look at Malcolm and crossed his arms. Miguel wasn't there to stop Malcolm this time. Bradley wanted to yell that together they could take Malcolm, but then what?

"Rick? Jon?" Danny asked.

Rick tried to hide behind Jon who moved back.

"Bradley, help me."

In a moment of madness, Bradley responded to Danny's plea and took one step forward. Twinges of pain shot out from his foot. He scrambled back to the safety of plane debris before Malcolm noticed. After all, the bully wasn't picking on him.

He told himself if the other boys hadn't been there he'd have stood up to Malcolm, but that was a lie. "Man up," his father loved to say, but he wasn't there.

Feeling the phone in his pocket, Bradley took it out. He needed to call for help, but who could he call? He didn't want another tongue-lashing from his father for being such a wimp that he couldn't take care of his own problems.

Not knowing who else to call, Bradley pocketed the phone and ran from the cover of plane debris into the bushes overlooking the beach.

"Leave me alone," Danny yelled. "You're crazy, all of you. No one will rescue us now."

"That's the point," Malcolm said. "Finish breaking the phones."

"Stop it." Danny pushed between Rick and Jon and ran up the beach.

"Lieutenant, sergeant-at-arms, bring him back," Malcolm yelled.

Danny scrambled up the hill. He slipped and pawed at the ground. The gang ran after him. No contest.

Bradley felt terrible, but he didn't dare stay. He could be next.

Danny screamed.

Bradley threw up. Then he ran along the shore away from the others.

THREE

Behind the cover of a large rock, Bradley caught his breath. Then he tilted his head back to take in rainwater to clear the taste in his mouth. The rains stopped. Clouds cast a twilight glow over the beach he'd left.

Danny's last words lingered. "I can't breathe."

Bradley's throat tightened, as if this was happening to him. He kept moving.

When Danny's groans stopped, Bradley almost felt relieved. They brought back memories of his mom's more muted moans in her last days, begging for it to end. But Bradley had felt Malcolm's anger before and didn't want to experience it again. He threw up, and couldn't get the taste out of his mouth.

Malcolm yelled, "Anyone else want to disobey me?"

Bradley snuck away, hoping this rocky island was big enough to find a hiding place. He reached a ridge with exposed rock and no cover to hide behind. He moved sideways around it. Behind him a light flashed, then three, heading his way.

"Come home, little Bradley," Malcolm said in the pretend-polite sing-song tone he used with Ms. Rose. "Come back before the she-devil gets you."

Stumbling, Bradley rolled down toward beach, banging his sore arm.

"Come out or you're dead," Malcolm bellowed, his voice sounding too close.

Bradley climbed up muddy rocks, banging his scraped knee. He stifled a yelp and kept going. When he reached the top of the ridge, he spotted the blonde girl again. Matted curls framed her sad face and sharp eyes. She beckoned for him to follow.

The lights following him split up. One headed along the beach. A second bobbed behind him. The third veered off to his left. He didn't want Danny's fate.

He climbed, following the girl, but he couldn't catch up with her. He cut his hands on rocks and stumbled. He landed on his bad knee again. Malcolm and his boys were gaining. Bradley got to his feet and ran.

Around a ridge, he spotted the girl, urging him to hurry. He lost his footing and rolled down into a ravine toward her. Thankfully, nothing new hurt. When he looked up, she was nearby and then disappeared behind rocks.

Bradley crawled across the muddy slope after her. He slipped and slid down a slippery incline. When he hit bottom, pain shot out from his foot. He stifled a scream. He was in a hole, looking up at the stormy sky.

The pit's floor was muddy and mucky, with whatever lived in the grimy depths. His first instinct was to climb out, but the hole was six feet deep and Malcolm was up there.

"Where'd our slimy Worm disappear to?" Malcolm yelled from above.

Bradley's pursuers could discover him by shining their lights down into the pit. Yet it wasn't just a pit. There was an opening, a shallow cave. Bradley squeezed inside. Lights flooded the pit. The girl's face lit up across from him, wild-eyed, mysterious, curls plastered against her cheeks. She hushed him.

"I don't see him," Jake said.

"Me either," Tony added.

The lights faded away. The pit went dark.

The girl had saved Bradley's life and he didn't even know her name. He crawled across the slippery pit to the opening where she'd crouched down. "Wait," he whispered.

Fearing Malcolm might overhear and grab him, Bradley crawled into a narrow tunnel that led away from the pit. The ground was slimy wet from the rain and black as his closet at home where he'd hid from his dad's rage, only to get another belting for hiding.

Bradley scraped his leg against the side of the tunnel and remembered the cell phone. He pulled it out, activated it, and could see the tunnel led upward. Holding the cell in his teeth, he crawled forward despite his fear of what waited for him. His fingers squished through the mud. The rotten odor caused his stomach to churn. He kept moving out of fear that Malcolm would find his footprints in the mud. Come morning they would be easy to spot.

The cell light went out. There was dim light up ahead. At first Bradley thought he'd gone in circles and was returning like a moth to Malcolm's flame. He couldn't risk lighting the phone again. Instead, he held his breath to listen and crept forward.

The crashing of waves against rocks grew louder. The light was coming through an opening that must have overlooked the sea. A shaft of light shone through an ivy-covered opening into a small cave. He crawled out of the tunnel into the cave.

Spooked by a nearby presence, Bradley crawled back toward the tunnel. He stopped, caught his breath, and saw the girl in the shadows with a finger to her lips. He sat across from her. Waves broke below them.

Like back at the airport, his mind went blank. So much crowded Bradley's overworked brain that paralysis seized him. He started shaking.

Her eyes caught his attention. They'd lost the sadness from back at the airport. Even in the shadows, their intensity unnerved him. Her hands moved in an intricate dance as if she and Bradley shared a secret language.

Not understanding, he shrugged.

She looked disgusted, as his dad did when Bradley didn't catch on quickly enough.

He whispered, "I don't—"

She motioned for him to stop and pointed toward the opening, where Malcolm might be. Then she poked her head outside. She pulled her head in, put her hand over her mouth, and stabbed her finger at Bradley as she had at Coach Mack at the airport. She pointed for Bradley to stay and then vanished into the tunnel.

He didn't like feeling alone, except this was better than being with his dad or Malcolm.

* * *

Bradley couldn't stop shaking. Were Ms. Rose, Coach Mack, and some of the boys really dead? Despite years of Bible study he still couldn't fathom what death meant. One moment you're here. The next you're gone, somewhere hopefully better. When she was alive, Ms. Rose stood between Malcolm and what he wanted to do to Bradley. Coach Mack had patched him up. Now they were gone, like Bradley's mom.

Soon, he felt antsy sitting in the cave by himself. He parted the ivy and peered outside, taking in the salty sea air. The sky brightened. Waves crashed over rocks some thirty feet below the cave opening. The heights made him dizzy.

The cliff wall rose another ten feet above the opening. He couldn't see how to climb up. Besides, what if Malcolm or one of the other boys was waiting for him? He slipped back into the cave. The girl had returned with two branches about his height. She took a dark rock from her jeans pocket and began shaving an end of one of the sticks, sharpening it.

"What ya doing?" was the best he could manage. He felt stupid, slow-witted, like Malcolm often said.

Eyes wide, she pointed the stick at him with one hand and covered her mouth with the other. She tossed one of her sticks his way along with a black stone that looked like flint. It felt sharp like the rocks outside that had cut his hands. Now Bradley wished he'd paid closer attention at summer camp.

The girl showed him how to hold the stick and use the sharp end of the flint to shave off layers of wood to bring the stick to a point.

He didn't see the benefit of making a spear. They needed a grownup to rescue them. Did she know about her dad, if Coach Mack was her dad? He assumed such from the way she talked to him at the airport and from what Malcolm had said. After all, why else was she at the airport?

"How?" he started to ask.

She signaled him to shut up. He was glad she hadn't pointed her spear at him again.

When he finished sharpening his stick, she held out her hand. He passed her the sharpened spear. She smiled, nodded, and tossed it back. Now that her hair was dry, it bounced up as curls.

Making the spear with her gave him a distraction, a sense of doing something, but it couldn't block what Malcolm had done to Danny and Miguel. Still, just having her near was reassuring.

"I said throw him over." Malcolm's voice sounded like thunder above them.

When the words penetrated Bradley's fog, he began trembling.

His companion acted frantic. Carrying her spear, she crept from the entry to the tunnel and back. Danny's baggy shirt fell outside the opening, beyond the ivy. What crashed against the rocks was much heavier. *That could have been me.*

"Now the other one," Malcolm said.

Bradley stared in disbelief as a blue uniform fell from above: a man, the pilot. The body hit the water below with a thud. Bradley gripped the spear. His stomach churned. Sweat streamed down his neck.

He had hoped somehow that the pilot and co-pilot could have survived, despite how mangled the cockpit became and the explosion. Without them, there were no more adults to stop the bully. Bradley couldn't believe Miguel was gone, though sometimes even Miguel picked on the smaller boys to avoid a fight with Malcolm.

Bradley steamed. "Man up," his father would say. "Bullies take advantage of you if you don't man up." That was his only advice, which was why Bradley never told his dad about Malcolm, and why he couldn't call him for help.

"Toss the radio," Malcolm yelled, "and anything that links to the outside world."

"No!" Jake said.

"You want to join the pilot and Danny?"

"Make sense, Malcolm. After our adventure we want to be found."

"Why? Either the black box and the radio go over or you do."

"Fine, you don't have to be such a …"

Jake didn't finish his thought. Several electronic boxes tumbled past the cave opening.

"Good job, Lieutenant. Now let's find that grimy Little Worm."

FOUR

Bradley clung to his spear as if it could give him strength and protect him.

"We need food and water," Jake said from outside, his voice trailing away from the cliff's edge.

"Where's little Bradley?" Malcolm asked. "Whoever brings me Little Worm wins points."

"Hey," Tony said. "Maybe we could catch fish with the Little Worm."

Bradley shivered. Malcolm was a monster. A killer. Bradley had thought long and hard about why Tony and Jake followed Malcolm instead of standing up to him. The only thing that made sense was that while Malcolm's attention was on the smaller boys, on Bradley, he wasn't bothering Tony or Jake. That gave Bradley no comfort.

As soon as the voices faded away, the girl crawled out the cave entrance. She grabbed hold of the ivy, attached the spear to her belt, and pulled herself up. Bradley watched her scale the cliff face to the top.

Fighting his height-terror, Bradley looked down. Two bodies lay slumped over the rocks, splashed by the waves. The pilot had landed face down, with his head in the water. His body looked mangled as if his legs had snapped either in the crash or when he landed on the rocks. Blood pooled around his head. Danny lay on his back, his head bashed in. Two other boys lay on the rocks below. Bradley couldn't tell who. His gut churned, ready to make him throw up again, except there couldn't be anything left in his stomach.

Beside the bodies were bits of cell phones, electronics, and boxes. A charred orange box looked as if someone had hammered it, breaking it in two, and then set it on fire. A wave crashed in and carried part of it out to sea.

Above, the girl tipped her head for Bradley to follow. Feeling the cell phone still in his pocket, he slipped back into the cave. In the corner, he pulled away some loose stones and buried the phone.

Despite his fear of heights, Bradley's fear of being alone won out. He crawled through the opening and clung to the ivy. The girl signaled him to move faster. He locked eyes with her. It gave him the strength to stand on the cave ledge. When he grabbed hold of the vine, his hands were five feet from the top. *You can do this,* he said to himself by way of encouragement. *Just don't look down.*

He pulled himself up a foot and froze. His father's words rang in his ears, which got him trembling.

He climbed another foot and another. *Malcolm, what if he returns?*

Bradley looked down toward the cave opening. Big mistake. He immediately felt dizzy. Closing his eyes, he climbed another foot. He grabbed hold of the rocks above him and pulled himself up until he could see over the top. Lights danced in the distance, down toward the beach with all the debris. His companion moved away from the cliff's edge, motioning for him to hurry.

He didn't know what to make of the girl who hadn't spoken a word to him. She wasn't the she-devil Malcolm had talked about. She had, after all, saved Bradley's life. So far. Except when she'd shaken her spear at him, she looked too angelic to be a devil. Yet, those were the worst kind. They fooled you into betraying yourself, or so Malcolm had said. Bradley wondered if some other kind of she-devil was the cause of Malcolm's anger, maybe the social worker. But that wasn't his problem.

Realizing he couldn't stay on the cliff's edge, Bradley pulled himself up onto rocky ledge.

Grabbing hold of her spear, the girl darted across a clearing behind bushes. She motioned for Bradley to follow and hurried away from the cliff. He eyed the cliff's edge and their hidden cave below. Ignoring twinges of pain in his foot, he ran after her to a clearing made by the plane when it crashed. One of wings and its engine lay near the cockpit, charred. Thankfully, the rain had kept the fire from spreading.

Plane debris cluttered the path down to the beach where the boys had ended up. Light, filtered through thinning clouds, cast a ghostly glow to the plane's debris. What was left of the charred cockpit lay on its side.

The girl ran beyond the cockpit and crouched down. Staying low, Bradley joined her. He wished for an adult to protect them from Malcolm. The pilot was at the bottom of the cliff. It looked as if someone had taken a hammer to the cockpit and pulled out all the electronics from the shell. The dashboard was black with soot, maybe from the lightning strikes or the explosion.

The girl nodded for him to follow her away from the cockpit. Debris trails spread out like star bursts where pieces had flown through the shrubbery. She followed one, climbed over a rocky ledge, and crouched down where she could watch the beach.

Below her lay the co-pilot, her blonde hair matted against her thin face. Her blue uniform was soaked red. Bradley hadn't ever seen so much blood. His stomach threatened to rise up into his throat. She turned her head and looked up at him. "Can you find bandages, antibiotics?"

She was alive, and she was an adult. There was hope.

He looked for the girl but couldn't see her. "Where?"

"First aid kit. Beside pilot's seat."

She grabbed hold of Bradley's arm. "Don't tell the other boys."

"No, ma'am."

Bradley hurried to the cockpit watching for the girl and hoping the first aid kit had survived. All he found in the cockpit itself had turned black with soot. He didn't see anything worth saving, let alone bandages. Not wanting to disappoint the co-pilot, he checked the bushes nearby and found a crushed box with a small bottle of alcohol, bandages, and both antibiotic pills and ointment. He carried them back to her.

When he reached the co-pilot, she struggled to breathe. Was this how his mom had been before lung cancer took her? His eyes teared up at the memory.

"Tell me what to do," he said.

She dragged herself to sit up and held out her left arm. Bone stuck out. She needed a doctor.

"Pour some alcohol. Then put the ointment on the bandage and wrap it tight."

Hands shaking, he did as she asked, all the time feeling nauseated by all the blood. He taped the bandage. "Anything else?"

She gasped. "My left leg." With her good arm, she tugged at a tear in her pants, widening it to show him a gash.

He repeated what he'd done for her arm and was impressed she didn't cry out. He wanted to. It looked like she was in a lot of pain.

"Go before those boys catch you."

Go where, he wanted to ask.

"There he is," Malcolm yelled. "Grab the Little Worm."

Bradley got to his feet and half-ran half-limped the other way. Footsteps crashed all around him, his and the other boys. He couldn't see how many.

"Whoever brings me Little Worm gets rewarded," Malcolm yelled.

The co-pilot let out a scream that turned Bradley's blood to ice. He wanted to go back and help her. But he didn't stand a chance with Malcolm, Jake, and Tony chasing him. He kept running.

Off to his right he spotted the girl on a ledge. Fuming, she waved toward Jake as if to get his attention. Jake was running in her direction. She didn't flee, as if she wanted him to catch her.

Bradley didn't know what took hold of him. His heart pounding in his throat. Suddenly he felt energized, as if something had jolted him alive. He ran toward the girl. Doom was bearing down on him and he wasn't fleeing, wasn't trying to save himself. He couldn't let Jake hurt his new friend.

As Bradley moved into the open, Jake turned his way. "There you are, Little Worm." Jake parroted Malcolm and ran straight toward Bradley.

* * *

Bradley veered left and spotted Tony the Joker running right for him. Bradley couldn't outrun either boy. He definitely couldn't escape both. He ran as fast as he could to draw the boys away from the girl with no name.

When he looked back, he no longer saw the girl, but the boys were closing in. He jumped across to nearby rocks and slid into a ravine. Ignoring the pain radiating from his foot, he rolled to his feet. He no longer saw Jake. Instead, he heard the boy moan, gurgle something, and fall silent. With Tony not far behind, Bradley ran. The girl stood up ahead, waving for him to hurry. He made it to where she'd been standing and found the pit he'd fallen into earlier.

Bradley didn't see the Joker, though rustling came from Tony's direction. Bradley jumped into the pit, landing like a cat on all fours. His foot screamed out again. He tumbled onto his side and crawled into the slimy tunnel on his hands and knees. Ignoring the rotting smell, he scrambled through the mud. He slid out of the tunnel, into the cave, and almost out the entry, which led over the cliff and onto the rocks below. Bracing himself against a cave wall, he caught his breath.

The girl sat across from him, cradling her spear. Her face filled with more sadness than he thought a face could hold, more even than his mom's the last time he saw her before she went into the hospital.

Bradley hung his head. "I'm sorry. I tried to save her."

"It was mighty brave of you to stand up to that boy," she said, her first words. "Foolish, but brave."

"I'm Bradley."

"I know who you are. You can call me Monique. I suppose you've earned that."

"How did you get here, Monique?" He liked the sound of her name.

"We need to find water and food." She grabbed her spear, climbed out the entry, and up the ivy.

It seemed strange on an island surrounded by water to imagine dying of thirst, but salt water could make you sick. He poked his head out of the cave, looked down, and shook so much he almost fell. He clenched his fists until the nausea faded.

When he stuck he head out again and looked up, she was studying him, her head tilted to one side. Not wanting to disappoint her, he grabbed hold of the vines and pulled himself up, keeping his eyes on her instead of the rocks below. Before he reached the top of the cliff, she moved away. He climbed up over the cliff's rocky ledge and joined her in the bushes.

Now that the storm had passed, the sky brightened. But the eastern sky was dark. Soon twilight would close in around them like a blanket. The night might help them hide, but Malcolm had lights.

Bradley followed Monique through the bushes away

from the cliff with the cockpit to their right.

"We should help the co-pilot," he said after they crossed the debris clearing.

She hurried on.

He was stunned that she didn't stop to check on maybe the only adult still alive. The crash had banged up the co-pilot pretty badly. He wanted to give her more help. Not seeing the co-pilot where he'd left her, he hurried to catch up with Monique. When they neared the bottom of the hill, she turned inland and led him into a small cleft not far from the pit he'd fallen into.

Water bubbled up out of the ground. She filled her hands, washed away the mud, and filled them again. Then she drank.

"Shouldn't we boil this?" he asked.

"Boiling requires a fire," Monique said. "That would attract those boys."

He did as she did. The water didn't carry an odor and had a mineral taste that wasn't bad. She took more and so did he.

"Is Coach your dad?" he asked.

"Drink and let's go." She took another handful of water and sneaked down toward the beach. She picked up a long stick and handed it to him. "You should have brought yours. You'll need it."

"Where did you hide on the plane?" he asked. "I'll bet you snuck into the luggage area."

"Don't be daft." Taking the black stone from her pocket, she carved the tip of his stick into a spear and handed it to him. "Hold the spear like this to defend yourself. It makes a better weapon to scare than if you have to use it, but it helps to be prepared."

"For what?" He already knew. His knees wobbled thinking about it.

Beneath the darkening sky, lights from the other side of the island cast a halo over the crown of the hill.

"Come on," Monique said, "evening is a good time to

fish." She entered the water and washed mud off her clothes.

"But we can't see."

She splashed him. "Don't tell me you're afraid of a little water."

While he washed off the mud, he felt exposed, out in the open. "You couldn't have hidden in the restroom. You were in the office when I boarded. And the restroom landed on the beach."

"Are you going to yammer or catch dinner?" She speared a fish and held it up. "See?"

"That was amazing."

"You do it. Imagine where the fish will go, not where it is."

"I can't see," he said.

She glared at him. He speared the water several times, hitting nothing but rock and sand. She nailed another fish. He pointed to lights heading their way along the beach to their left. She led him the other way, up the hill to the cliff. When they reached the top, she stopped in a clearing overlooking the sea and showed him how to use her gray stone to slice the fish open and remove the bones.

Bradley was mesmerized watching her work. She sliced her sharp stone along the fish's belly as if she'd done this a thousand times.

"Did you sneak into the cockpit?" he asked. He couldn't see how since the door had been right in front of him.

"All you need to survive is water, food, shelter, and a way to defend yourself." She demonstrated how to throw the spear. "That'll buy you time."

"You're not going to tell me, are you?"

"Eat up."

"You have a twin sister," he guessed. But that didn't explain how she knew him.

She smiled. Threads of moonlight reflected in her eyes, giving her a wraithlike appearance. She handed him half of a fish. "Eat before your friends return."

"They're not my friends."

"Obviously."

Bradley sniffed at the fish. It had a strong, oily odor. He turned up his nose at eating uncooked fish.

Like his mom used to, Monique encouraged him to eat up. It didn't taste like the cans of tuna his dad forced him to eat. He swallowed quickly because Monique was almost finished.

As they ate, pinpoints of light moved around the island from the beach where they'd fished, up over the crown, and toward the first beach. Now they moved toward the cliff.

"Time to go," she said.

"Shouldn't we rescue the co-pilot?"

"We can't. They moved her."

"What about Jake," Bradley asked, "the one who ran after you?"

Monique wiped her hands on a leafy bush and scrambled down the vine over their cave.

Bradley counted three lights—no two. One was a single stick with lights on both ends. Malcolm had all the lights and yelled at what looked like three figures dragging something uphill toward the cliff.

Moonlight shifted. No, the boys did. Tony the Joker was dragging something. Rick's glasses reflected the light. He and Jon pulled something else. Despite being terrified, Bradley wanted a better look.

"Psst." Monique's voice came from the cliff's edge.

He crawled and looked down in time to see her scoot into the cave. He was thankful he couldn't see the rocks below. He started down and hung on the ledge until the lights approached the clearing. The boys were dragging two bodies. Jon dropped Coach Mack's head.

Malcolm shoved Jon to the ground. "Listen, you fat pig. Pick him up."

Tony dragged Miguel by the arms. The head hung like a

floppy dishrag. "Do we have to do this? It's not funny anymore."

"Yeah, you have to. Get moving." Malcolm shined his light toward the cliff's edge.

* * *

Bradley slid down the vines and climbed into the cave. The moment he was inside, light shined over the cliff at the breaking waves. His stomach heaved at the thought that he'd been climbing down the cliff, above the bodies of the pilot, Danny, and two other boys.

"I have something for you," Monique said.

For a moment he'd forgotten she was there. He didn't want her to see him this way, helpless as a newborn baby. He swallowed hard and pulled away from the opening.

She sat across from him. Malcolm's light off the cliff reflected shadows on her face. She put a finger to her lips and pointed up. Then she handed Bradley a large bronze coin. He moved closer to the opening to see it better. The coin was an award for excellence in mountain climbing. He felt ashamed that he didn't know as much about how to survive as she did.

"Thanks," he whispered.

She covered her mouth and wagged her finger at him. He nodded. Malcolm was above them.

"He's too heavy." Jon's strained voice came from outside.

"You should exercise more," Malcolm said. "Drag him over to the edge."

Through the ivy, Bradley saw part of the cliff face nearby. Afraid of being seen, he drew back.

"Pick it up," Malcolm said.

"Shouldn't we say something," Jon said. "He was our coach."

Bradley flinched as Coach Mack's body fell past the opening. Jon let loose a curdling scream. Coach hit the rocks with a thud. Jon fell past the opening, his arms flailing. He cried out and gurgled.

"Jon?" Rick said. "Why'd you do that? You're crazy. No! NO!"

"Crazy, huh," Malcolm said. "We'll see about that."

He must have pushed Rick. The smaller boy screamed all the way to the rocks below. Bradley wanted to look and not look at the same time. He didn't want to be next.

"You didn't have to do that," Tony said. "He wasn't going to tell anyone."

"Now he won't for sure," Malcolm said. "Let's find our Little Worm. He has to be around here somewhere."

"We should look for Rick," Tony said.

"Not until we have Bradley."

FIVE

Bradley waited until the voices above faded away. Then he poked his head out of the cave into darkness. Waves broke against the rocks below. He couldn't see the bodies. He'd lost track of how many were there.

For the longest time he strained to see, until his eyes ached as much as his heart. He hated feeling helpless. He hadn't stood up for Danny. He hadn't tried to stop Malcolm from pushing Rick and Jon over the cliff. He couldn't even save the co-pilot.

He settled into the cave, no longer able to feel Monique's presence. Being alone in the dark spooked him.

Bradley forced air into his lungs, stale with whatever had lived and decayed in this cave. He hoped it was birds or small mammals, something that wouldn't harm him. But the odor of the cave mixed with the smell of the fish to make him feel it was coming from the bodies on the rocks below. He didn't want to be alone on a night like this. He certainly didn't want Malcolm hurting Monique.

He felt his way around the cave to the tunnel. Dragging his spear with him, he crawled along the foul tunnel to the pit. Moving made him feel less helpless.

Monique wasn't in the pit when he got there. There

was no sound of anyone nearby, so he climbed the rocky side of the pit and hid in the bushes. The clouds had thinned, allowing moonlight to poke through.

A single light lit up Tony's face and moved from the cliff down toward the pit. Then it disappeared. Either that or Tony had turned it off. The light reappeared, moving down toward Bradley. He dropped lower to the ground and was plunged into darkness.

When he looked up, a brighter double light hung near the cockpit, not moving. Bradley held tight to his spear and prepared to jump into the pit. Moonlight caught Monique's curls. She appeared on a ledge above him as if she could see him clear as daylight. She held out her spear, turned, and hurried up toward the cliff.

Bradley carried his spear like a walking stick and followed. Monique ran, disappearing ahead of him. He reached the top of the hill. The cliff was to his right. The double light was not far from where the cockpit had landed.

Not seeing Monique or the single light anywhere, he moved toward the cockpit, curious as to why the double-light hadn't moved. Malcolm was hunting him, the Little Worm, yet he wasn't moving. Was he lying in wait?

Bradley slid down a slippery patch and stepped on something soft and squishy. When he looked down he gasped and fell backward into bushes.

Tony the Joker was face down, a stake through his chest. In the moonlight, it looked like one of his comical pranks, except blood pooled around his shirt. The stake looked like it broke off a spear. *Monique?*

Not knowing whether to be impressed or petrified, Bradley was both. She'd been there when Jake had disappeared as well. His heart raced, jumping into his throat. She was a mountain girl. She'd given him the medallion so he would know. She knew how to survive out here.

* * *

Bradley heard groaning nearby. Trembling, he shook loose from his imaginings. He held the spear as Monique had showed him and moved toward the light. Up ahead, poking out from the shadows along the path, he saw blonde curls on the ground. He tasted vomit. The spear shook in his hand. Still, he moved closer and listened for Monique's screams.

She didn't make a sound. But Malcolm did, grunting with exertion, his hands around the blonde's neck.

Gripping his only weapon, Bradley inched forward. He imagined Danny after he stopped screaming. And the others. *No!*

As if possessed by the devil herself, Bradley charged into the light. "Leave her alone, you monster." He looked down to where the blonde lay, but couldn't see Monique through his tears.

Malcolm rolled away from the body and stood up. "Little Worm grows a spine. You think that makes you a man?"

Bradley's trembling hand shook the spear. His eyes burned. He wiped them and started to charge the bigger boy. "Be a man," his father would say.

Malcolm raised a stick. "Argh." He jumped up and down, puffing out his chest like a baboon.

"Run. Get out of here," Bradley yelled to Monique.

"She's not going anywhere and neither are you," Malcolm said. "It's just you and me. Man and Worm." He threw the stick, hitting Bradley's bruised arm.

Stepping back, Bradley fell over debris. He steadied himself, trying to recall what Monique had said about holding and throwing the spear. He would only get one shot. His hands were shaking too much to aim well.

"I'm going to enjoy tearing you to pieces, Little Worm." Malcolm picked up another stick and threw it.

Bradley ducked. "Run," he shouted to Monique. "Hide somewhere."

"There's nowhere to hide on this tiny island. That's the beauty of it. You're as good as dead."

"You can't scare me," Bradley said.

The sly smile returned to Malcolm's face. "You'll still die like the others. Poor scared Little Worm."

Malcolm threw a stone, hitting Bradley's head. When Malcolm bent over to pick up something else to throw, Bradley threw the spear. It grazed Malcolm's back and slid away. Bradley ran toward the cliff.

Malcolm was right. Bradley didn't know how to fight. He wasn't a killer. Yet if he didn't end this, Malcolm would.

Bradley didn't want to give up the hideout, but if he didn't get away from Malcolm, it wouldn't matter. He tried to locate where to climb down.

The bigger boy gave chase. "You can't hide from me. No one can. Stop and I'll let you be my slave for the night." He was gaining on the Little Worm.

Outlined by rays of moonlight, Monique knelt on the cliff. She climbed over the edge. She'd gotten away. But it made no sense. She was motionless on the ground. Malcolm was hurting her. Now he was after the Little Worm.

Bradley etched the spot in his mind where Monique had knelt and ran as fast as he could.

"Where you going, Little Worm? You going to jump? Maybe you should."

Bradley found the spot, dropped to the ground, and grabbed hold of the vines. Malcolm was a mere ten feet behind. On the ground behind the brute was a head with blonde curls. That had to be the co-pilot.

Bradley shimmied down to the cave entrance. As soon as he had his feet on the ledge leading into their hideout, light blazed down from above. He dropped down another foot and tried to remember how he'd climbed in before.

Malcolm set the light down and began to cut at the ivy

with the knife he'd taken from Miguel. Bradley lifted his feet and swung them over the ledge and into the cave entrance. Malcolm stopped cutting to throw stones. Bradley flinched and dodged aside. Before he fell onto the rocks below, he pulled himself into the cave. The last thing he saw before he was inside was Malcolm grabbing the vines to climb down.

"You can't escape," Malcolm said. "I've got you now, scared Little Worm."

Bradley crawled backward into the cave. Once he was inside, Monique handed him her spear. Nodding, he braced himself and grabbed hold of the weapon. He placed the point toward the entrance as Malcolm rappelled down the vines. First came the feet. Then the big boy's face hung over the opening. He shined a light inside and stared at the spear.

"You're not man enough," Malcolm said.

Trembling, Bradley jabbed the point at the bigger boy.

Malcolm kicked away from the cliff to avoid the strike. The force of his push and his weight snapped the partly-cut vines. Scrambling up the falling stems, he let the light tumble to the rocks below. He wailed like a baby all the way down. His landing came with a thud and sounded like the snapping of twigs.

Bradley peered down at waves breaking over the rocks, lit by a double-sided light. Malcolm stared up with vacant eyes. His right arm twitched as if he were shaking his fist. Then it stopped. Around him were eleven other bodies.

SIX

Bradley withdrew into the cave. Monique was gone. He liked how strong and tomboyish she was, though not how she disappeared, leaving him alone. He didn't go after her. He'd had far too much excitement for one day, for a lifetime. Besides, she knew how to get by in the wild. He curled up by the cave entrance with the spear in his hand and kept watch until his eyes refused to stay open.

He woke to light entering the cave. Monique sat, watching him. He got up and bumped his head, which hurt from the night before. He rubbed his scalp but the real ache was inside.

"It's time for you to go," she said.

"Go where?"

"A helicopter landed. They're searching for survivors."

"They found us?" he said. "That's great. Wait, aren't you coming?"

"I can't. But you should hurry before they leave."

"The vine is gone."

"The tunnel," she said. "Come on. I'll see you off."

"We've only just met."

She smiled. "That's sweet. Now go."

Bradley followed her through the tunnel and out of the

pit. The smell didn't bother him now that it was daylight and rescuers had come. Dozens of men and women in bright orange uniforms spread out searching.

"I'll never forget you," Monique said. "Go. It would be best if you didn't tell them about me."

"Are you …"

"Am I what?"

"Malcolm said you were a she-devil," Bradley said.

"What do you think?" She pointed toward the beach.

"I don't want to leave. I like you."

"Go on, no more fuss." She dropped into the pit. "Go."

Before Bradley could jump in after her, an orange uniformed arm grabbed him.

"Careful there," a man's voice said. He pulled Bradley away from the pit. "You got a name, son?"

"Bradley Munsch." He eyed the pit, but Monique had vanished.

"I'm Captain Tunney. We're here to take you home."

Bradley shrugged. He didn't want to go home to a father who thought him a sissy. He wanted to stay with Monique.

"We would have arrived sooner," the captain grumbled, "but the plane's transponder and black box stopped signaling. Luckily, we were able to triangulate off a cell phone signal. Where is everyone?"

Bradley's gut churned. He couldn't stop trembling at the memories. "Malcolm dumped bodies off the cliff."

"Malcolm Jones?"

Bradley nodded.

The captain put his arm around the boy. "Where is he now?"

Shivering at the memory, Bradley pointed toward the cliff. "You have to save my friend, Monique."

"Monique? Why don't you slow down and start at the beginning."

* * *

Bradley finished telling Captain Tunney his story.

"So you're the only survivor?" the captain asked.

"I tried to bandage the co-pilot," Bradley said, recalling her broken arm, "but Malcolm found her."

"I'm sorry. Being alone during all this must have been quite upsetting."

"I had Monique."

A soldier with sergeant stripes approached. "You've got to see this." He pointed up toward the cliff.

"The boy told me. Any survivors?"

The sergeant shook his head. "We've scoured the island using infrared and motion sensors."

"What about Monique?" Bradley asked. "She has to be here."

"There's no one by that name on the passenger list," the soldier said. "And we've accounted for thirteen boys and four adults."

"I swear. She's here," Bradley said. "I think she's Coach McDonald's daughter."

"McDonald and your co-pilot have a daughter named Megan," the captain said. "No Monique."

That twisted Bradley's innards. He choked to think of Megan wanting to come with her parents and losing them both. Tears filled his eyes. Then it hit him. Monique had to be Megan. She knew him and he'd seen her at the airport. She was the girl Malcolm said was Coach's daughter. "Maybe she snuck into the cockpit."

"No room," the captain said. "Look, we need to get you home."

"But Monique?"

"Excuse me." Captain Tunney took the sergeant uphill, away from Bradley, and whispered. "Between the crash and hiding from Malcolm Jones, we shouldn't be surprised the boy has become delusional about an imaginary friend."

Bradley's ears perked up as the winds blew his way.

"I'll keep an eye on him," the sergeant said.

"Thanks."

"Is it true what they're saying that there's a warrant for Malcolm's arrest, for assaulting a woman yesterday?"

The captain nodded. "Allegedly he attacked the social worker checking up on a report that Malcolm had put his own mother in the hospital last month."

"Maybe it's a blessing he's gone."

"Except now we won't get answers.

* * *

The sergeant buckled Bradley into one of two military helicopters on the beach where the fuselage had come to rest.

Bradley wanted to find Monique, but she didn't want to be found. And she knew how to hide. That made him smile. She'd saved his life. He owed her. If that meant letting her go, he had to give her that.

Through the open door, he overheard two orange-uniformed soldiers talking outside.

"What did you say they call this island?" one soldier asked.

"An Aussie named it Sheila Rock," another soldier said. "Some call it She-devil Rocks. Quite a few boats have crashed on these shores. There's no fresh water. No one can live here for long."

"So Malcolm went on a rampage before falling off the cliff last night."

"Looks like it," the second soldier said. "If I had to wager, I'd say he caused this crash to avoid getting arrested. Then he killed himself. I do find it curious that one of the boys fell into a ravine, stabbing himself on the branch of a thorny bush and another fell into a pit, breaking his neck.

"She-devil Rocks about sums it up, then."

As they lifted off, Bradley plastered his face against the window. The island was small with a few trees, scrubby vegetation, and few places to hide. Except Monique had found water, food, and a cave to escape Malcolm. Bradley felt terrible that he couldn't save the co-pilot. If Monique was Megan then his new friend had lost both her parents.

Monique had been the best friend he'd ever had.

The helicopter lifted and flew south. Bradley spotted a lone figure on the cliff. Her blond hair blew in the wind. She held a spear in each hand, which she raised in salute.

He started to point her out for the sergeant but decided against turning her in. As he shifted in his seat, the medallion dug into his leg. He reached into his pocket and clutched the token Monique had given him.

I will return for you.

OTHER STORIES BY LANCE ERLICK

REGINA SHEN: RESILIENCE (Regina Shen book 1)

Outcast Regina Shen is forced by the World Federation to live on the seaward side of barrier walls built to hold back rising seas from abrupt climate change. A hurricane threatens to destroy what's left of her world, tearing Regina from her family.

Global fertility has collapsed. Chief Inspector Joanne Demarco of the notorious Department of Antiquities believes Regina holds the key to avoid extinction. Regina fights to stay alive and avoid capture while hunting for her family. Does she have the resilience to survive?

REGINA SHEN: VIGILANCE (Regina Shen book 2)

Regina Shen is pursued by the notorious Department of Antiquities for her unique DNA. She jumps the Barrier Wall into the Federation to find her kidnapped sister. Stuck on a heavily-guarded closed-university campus in the mountains, she must use her wits to escape and rescue her sister without letting either of two rival Antiquities inspectors capture her.

REGINA SHEN: DEFIANCE (Regina Shen book 3)

Outcast Regina Shen has DNA the Federation believes can reverse a global fertility collapse. Rival Federation agents fight over capturing Regina to gain power amidst turmoil over who will become the new World Premier. Regina has to flee from Virginia through desert and wilderness to Alaska to hunt a treasure big enough to barter for her freedom and that of her sister.

THE REBEL WITHIN (Rebel Series book 1)

Annabelle Scott lives under the iron rule of a female-dominated régime that forces males to fight to the death to train the military elite. When pressed into service as a mechanized warrior to capture escaped boys, Annabelle stays true to herself by helping some escape. Her defiance endangers everyone she loves and thrusts her to a place of impossible life and death decisions.

THE REBEL TRAP (Rebel Series book 2)

Despite being a military recruit, Annabelle Scott rebels against her female-dominated régime by refusing to kill a handsome boy she fancies and helping him escape. Auditory implants and cameras allow her commander to watch her 24-7. Can she help the boy free his brother from a heavily-guarded geek institute without destroying her family or getting killed?

REBELS DIVIDED (Rebel Series book 3)

The first time Geo sees Annabelle, they meet as enemies and she doesn't kill him, which mystifies them both. It's after the 2nd Civil War with the nation divided into an all-female Federal Union and a warlord controlled Outland. The Outland warlord kidnaps Annabelle's sister and kills Geo's pa. Can Annabelle and Geo overcome mutual distrust and work together to rescue her sister and gain justice for his pa's murder? And will their feelings for each other derail or further their goals?

MAIDEN VOYAGE (short story)

Security Chief Nina Rekovic keeps the peace on the all-female Maiden's Ark that left Earth five years before. Distress signal says Earth is lost, stranding lunar colonists. Someone sabotages the vital fertility lab. While balancing Returners she sympathizes with, a dictatorial captain, and an estranged lover who betrays her, can Rekovic solve the conspiracy before she's imprisoned or worse?

WATCHING YOU (short story)

At the intersection of pervasive networks and the Patriot Act, we have the ability and some say the obligation to know everything about everyone. Can privacy survive? Can the individual endure?

Harold is a second-class citizen and a low-level worker in a government surveillance system charged with reviewing "criminal activity." He has private thoughts about a woman he's forbidden from approaching. He will not be deterred.

ABOUT THE AUTHOR

Lance Erlick likes to explore the mysteries of intriguing worlds with interesting, often strong female guides facing and overcoming adversity as they try to change their world. He hopes readers will enjoy his writing as they discover different worlds, going places they may never have been.

He writes science fiction thrillers, appealing to young adult and adult readers. He is the author of *The Rebel Within*, *The Rebel Trap*, and *Rebels Divided*, three books in the Rebel series. In those stories, he explores the consequences of following conscience for those coming of age. He authored the Regina Shen series—*Regina Shen: Resilience, Regina Shen: Vigilance*, and *Regina Shen: Defiance*. This series takes place after abrupt climate change leads to the Great Collapse and a new society under the World Federation. A related short story is: *Regina Shen: Into the Storm*. Lance is also the author of unrelated short stories: *Maiden Voyage* and *Watching You*.

Find out more about the author and his work at LanceErlick.com. Go to that website to sign up to receive occasional email newsletters with links to free short stories, and updates on new releases and other writing developments.

www.ingramcontent.com/pod-product-compliance
Lightning Source LLC
Chambersburg PA
CBHW071217130626
46555CB00004B/1740